I FORGOT

Story and Pictures by
SUÇIE STEVENSON

ORCHARD BOOKS　New York & London

A division of Franklin Watts, Inc.

Orchard Books, 387 Park Avenue South, New York, New York 10016
Orchard Books Great Britain, 10 Golden Square, London W1R 3AF England
Orchard Books Australia, 14 Mars Road, Lane Cove, New South Wales 2066
Orchard Books Canada, 20 Torbay Road, Markham, Ontario 23P 1G6

Orchard Books is a division of Franklin Watts, Inc.

Manufactured in the United States of America. Book design by Mina Greenstein
The text of this book is set in 16 pt. Aster. The illustrations are watercolor, reproduced in full
color.   10   9   8   7   6   5   4   3   2   1

Library of Congress Cataloging-in-Publication Data
Stevenson, Suçie. I forgot: story and pictures/by Suçie Stevenson. Summary: Although Arthur the
platypus has a terrible time remembering everything from his hat to the names of the oceans, he
finds that there are some important things in his life which he can remember.
[1. Memory—Fiction.   2. Platypus—Fiction.]   I. Title.   PZ7.S8483Iab   1988
[E]—dc19   87-22991   CIP   AC
ISBN 0-531-05744-5.   ISBN 0-531-08344-6 (lib. bdg.)

TO PETER

Whatever he was told to remember

ZiiNG

Arthur always forgot.

"Did you wash your
face, Arthur?"

"Oops!"

Then he forgot which kind of hat.

**Off to school at last
Arthur met Nancy from next door.**

"What's with the hat, Arthur?"

Nancy was practicing the names of the oceans.

"...Arctic
...Atlantic
...Indian...
What's next, Arthur?"

"Huh?"

"Where's your lunchbox,
Arthur?"

"Forgot it!
I'll be right back,
Elwin..."

The next day Arthur forgot . . .

...it was a school day

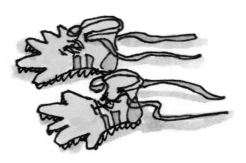

...his sneakers

...his sandwich for lunch

...his pencil with an eraser for arithmetic

...what time it was.

His mother and father gave him a talk...

So Arthur t-r-i-e-d remembering . . .

"Monday,
Tuesday,
Wednesday...
uh...
un...
Friday?"

"A, B, C, D,
E, F, G, H...
H...
K...O...
P...
WXYZ!"

"Arctic,
Atlantic,
Persifit...
Persikif...?"

He practiced and practiced.

HE TRIED REMINDERS...

...wearing a
rubber band
on his wrist...

SNAP

"Ouch!"

"Maybe if I just
stretch it out
enough..."
BOING

...tying
colored string
to his flippers...

He tried notes.

He really tried.
But nothing worked.

Outside, Arthur stared up at the sky...